J.J. Moorman

The Ohio White Sulphur Springs

Anatiposi

J.J. Moorman

The Ohio White Sulphur Springs

Reprint of the original, first published in 1859.

1st Edition 2023 | ISBN: 978-3-38231-302-9

Anatiposi Verlag is an imprint of Outlook Verlagsgesellschaft mbH.

Verlag (Publisher): Outlook Verlag GmbH, Zeilweg 44, 60439 Frankfurt, Deutschland
Vertretungsberechtigt (Authorized to represent): E. Roepke, Zeilweg 44, 60439 Frankfurt, Deutschland
Druck (Print): Books on Demand GmbH, In de Tarpen 42, 22848 Norderstedt, Deutschland

THE

OHIO WHITE SULPHUR SPRINGS,

BY

J. J. MOORMAN, M. D.,

Resident Physician at the White Sulphur Springs, Va.; Author of the "Virginia
Springs, and the Springs of the South and West," etc., etc.

WITH

Observations at the Ohio White Sulphur,

IN 1858,

By W. W. DAWSON, M. D.,

Formerly Professor of Anatomy and Physiology in the Cincinnati College of
Medicine and Surgery.

CINCINNATI:
MOORE, WILSTACH, KEYS & CO., PRINTERS,
25 WEST FOURTH STREET.
1859.

Ohio White Sulphur Springs,

SITUATED ON THE SCIOTO RIVER, EIGHTEEN MILES NORTH
OF COLUMBUS, TEN MILES FROM DELAWARE, AND
FIVE MILES FROM WHITE SULPHUR STATION,
ON THE SPRINGFIELD, MT. VERNON
AND PITTSBURGH RAILROAD.

———

THE OHIO WHITE SULPHUR SPRINGS will be
opened for visitors on the 1st of JUNE, and will be closed
about the 1st of OCTOBER.

The great want of a first-class Watering-Place in the West
has induced the Proprietor to spare no exertion or expense
calculated to make these Springs worthy of the most entire
confidence, and he feels that, as a delightful retreat during
the summer months, they have now few rivals in the
country; but, as of most importance, it is to the *Medicinal
qualities of these Waters*, as given in the papers of Drs. Moorman and Dawson, that he would particularly direct the
attention of all—more especially that of invalids.

☞ For "Railroad Relations of the Springs," and "Improvements of 1859," see Appendix.

THE

OHIO WHITE SULPHUR SPRINGS.

———————

NEAR the geographical center of Ohio, in the county of Delaware, and immediately on the western bank of the Scioto river, surrounded by a country broken, hilly, and beautifully picturesque, arises the OHIO WHITE SULPHUR.

The Scioto is here a rippling, rapid stream, hastily flowing and fretting over beds of boulder rocks, and skirted, for many miles above and below the Springs, by slopes or banks of considerable elevation, which gently spread out into undulatory table lands, charmingly interspersed with valley and hill, and blessed with an atmosphere free from malarious influences, at every season of the year—and as salubrious as is found in our high mountain ranges.

Under the name of *Hart's Springs*, this place has been known for its mineral waters for more than twenty years. The circumstance which led to its improvement as a Spring-property, by Mr. Hart, its former proprietor, is worthy of note. He had visited the White Sulphur Springs in Virginia, for the relief of a complicated stomach and liver complaint; returning to Ohio, cured of his disease, his attention was called to this Artesian Sulphur fountain, and upon examination, he found its waters so strikingly to resemble those of the Virginia spring as to induce him to purchase and improve it in view of its medicinal value.

The property has recently been purchased by Mr. A. WILSON, of Cincinnati, whose energy, good taste, and ample means, are being actively exercised in enlarging its accommodations, and still further beautifying the place, already by the beauties of nature surprisingly beautiful.

The buildings, for visitors, are pleasantly situated on a beautifully undulating plateau, at an elevation perhaps of one hundred and twenty feet above the level of the river, and about eight hundred feet distant from it. With those now in progress to completion, the accommodation will be ample and comfortable, for six hundred persons. The *drawing* of the grounds, including the various improvements on the Spring Lawn, that accompanies this article, renders a particular description of them unnecessary.

The good taste and liberality of the proprietor
of this property seem to be untiring in suggest-
ing and carrying forward new means of comfort
and amusement for his visitors, as well as for the
more beneficial use of the waters. To these ends
a charming wood-lawn, of a hundred acres, adjoining the Spring-lawn, has been laid off in
walks and carriage-drives; and extensive *Bathing-
houses* have been erected, furnishing not only
warm and *hot* tub-baths, but also with arrangements for employing *douche* and *sweat* baths:
these can not fail from the high mineral impreg-
nation of the water, to prove eminently valuable
in a great variety of cases.

The construction of *douche* and *sweating* baths
of sulphur water, to be employed under proper
circumstances, in connection with the internal
use of the water, is a matter of the utmost importance to the successful treatment of numerous
cases that resort to mineral springs.

The water for bathing, is here heated by *steam*,
in the tub in which it is used. This is a vast
improvement over the old method of heating
mineral waters for bathing. Under the old plan
of heating in a boiler, and thence conveying the
water to the bathing-tub, much of its valuable
saline matter was precipitated and lost. By this

improved method of applying steam to the water in the tub, the heat is never so great in raising the water to the bathing point, as to cause any important precipitation of its salts—hence they are left in their natural suspension in the water, to exert their specific effect upon the bather. Not only so, by this improved method, hot steam may be let into the tub, from time to time, as the water cools, so as to keep it essentially of the same temperature during the entire process of bathing—a consideration often of no small importance. This method of heating mineral waters, in the tub in which they are used, in connection with *douche* and *sweating* baths, brings warm and hot bathing at this place in fair competition with bathing at naturally warm and hot springs, and will be productive of the same good effects that are experienced from bathing in such springs.

The Ohio White Sulphur fountain is a curiosity in hydraulics. Its waters arise in a boring made through solid rock, that underlies the bed of the river, and are thrown up by subterranean power, one hundred and sixty feet, to the surface of the earth, where a pipe is attached to the mouth of the boring or well, along which, by means of the same subterranean power, they are propelled a distance of more than three hundred feet, and to an elevation of some sixty feet above the level of the river. Here they flow into a beautiful marble reservoir—the fountain from which the water is received for drinking. From the base of this reservoir, the water is conducted under ground to the *Bath-rooms*, and from thence to form a beautiful *jet d'eau* in its exit to the river, into which it falls when released from its utilitarian purposes.

A hydrodynamic problem here very naturally arises in the inquisitive mind. By what power is this volume of water made to rise more than two hundred feet perpendicularly, above its source in the bowels of the earth?

Writers on physics assert, that there are but two known forces that account for such phenomena: first, a gaseous force; and it is alleged that when water is propelled by such a force, it always flows more or less *per saltum*, and not in a constant, regular stream: second, on the well-known force or principle, by which water finds its own level. Now, this water does not come up *per saltum*, in any degree, but in a continuous, bold, dashing current. When we look around in search of a probable elevation from which it might come, we find it not in the State of Ohio, nor in many hundreds of miles in any direction, except in the great Appalachian chain of Virginia or Pennsylvania—and the nearest of these perhaps two hundred miles distant. Do these sulphur waters, as such, come from the great Alleghany supplies that are known to exist, and are so frequently found issuing from the base of that range of mountains in Virginia; or do they receive their mineral impregnations near the place where they arise, and is there some force not yet understood, by which water may be propelled to great hights above its natural source? Interesting as this question may be, we must leave its ultimate decision to those more deeply versed in the arcana of nature than ourselves.

This fountain, as valuable as a medicinal agent as it is curious in physics, was first discovered about thirty-four years ago. A gentleman by the name of Bachus, was boring at this place for salt water, and after penetrating the solid rock to the depth of one hundred and sixty feet, his auger suddenly sunk two feet, and the sulphur water gushed out. Not then appreciating the value of this discovery, he continued his boring —still through solid rock—to the further depth of three hundred and thirty feet, where he reached salt water, but not of sufficient strength to justify its evaporation into salt, as a business. Subsequently the lower boring was plugged, and the sulphur water alone permitted to flow up.

The hole along which the water rises is seven and a half inches in circumference, up which it rushes with tremendous force, at the rate of one hundred and twenty gallons a minute, or seven thousand two hundred gallons per hour.

To convey some idea of the volume of this subterranean current of sulphur water, and the rapidity with which it is forced along its channel, we are told, that an attempt was made to introduce a copper tube from the surface to the bottom of the well, and that very soon that portion of the tube that entered the current, became bent and flattened by its force.

Although these springs have but for a few years attracted much of public attention, enough is satisfactorily known of them to enable us to welcome them to a prominent position among the watering-places of the country.

Their geographical position—being central in the great and flourishing State in which they are situated, and essentially so as between the population of the South-west, and the watering-places of the Middle and Northern States—the ready facility by which they are approached by Railroad, from every direction, and above all, the medicinal value of their waters point them out as a place of very large valetudinary and fashionable resort by the people of America. So fortunately are they located in reference to accessibility, that visitors from North, South, East, or West, can approach within five miles of them on unbroken chains of Railroad.

The elevated and healthful country in which they are situated, with the established fact of its entire freedom from malarious influences, at all seasons of the year, give to persons who are seeking a healthful climate for a summer retreat a reliable assurance of finding such at this place.

The waters of this sulphur fountain have been analyzed by Professor E. S. Wayne, of Cincinnati, who shows that their gaseous contents consist of

Sulphureted Hydrogen,	Carbonic Acid.

Their solid contents of

Sulphate of Lime,	Carbonate of Lime,
Sulphate of Magnesia,	Oxide of Iron,
Chloride of Calcium,	Sulphate of Calcium,
Chloride of Sodium,	Iodine,
Chloride of Magnesium,	Organic Matter.

Their temperature, winter and summer, is uniformly 52° Fahrenheit.

This analysis shows that the water holds in solution many of the best ingredients found in the most celebrated waters of Europe and America, and indicates its adaptation to a large circle of chronic diseases to which humanity is subject.

Whilst this water strikingly resembles the Virginia White Sulphur in several respects, it is still more like the waters of Avon and Sharon, in New York, than any other with which I am familiar. The two latter waters differ somewhat from each other, and so will this be found to differ from both; nevertheless the likeness is not inapt between them in many essential particulars.

The author visited, and spent some time at these springs in 1857, and again in 1858, with the view of examining the waters, and ascertaining by scientific research, and practical observation, their peculiar characteristics and medical adaptations. The field of observation, while at the springs, was too limited to mature conclusions as definite and positive, in reference to the specific character of the waters, as was desirable; but in all cases in which I witnessed their use, the effects were highly satisfactory; and many intelligent persons, among them medical men of high reputation, who had used the waters, assured me of their beneficial effects. ·But want of observation upon my part has been fully supplied by

Dr. W. W. Dawson, of Cincinnati, a gentleman of science and learning in his profession, who spent the entire summer of 1858 at the springs. In his "*Observations at the Ohio White Sulphur Springs*"* (published entire in this pamphlet), he gives a clear and satisfactory account of the curative powers of the waters in *Dyspepsia*, and the various depravities of the stomach; in diseases of the *Liver*, and in various chronic affections of the bowels and kidneys.

Dr. Dawson reports a very interesting case of *Chronic Pericarditis*, that was entirely cured by the water.

He recommends its use in *congestion* of the lungs and tracheal tubes. In a case of *Chlorosis*, that came under his observation, it was signally successful; and decided benefit was derived from its employment in cases of Dropsical effusions.

Dr. D. informs us, he had but little opportunity of seeing the waters tested in Rheumatism, or in severe affections of the skin; but from my observations of the value of similar waters in those diseases, I should have great confidence in their use in such cases; especially when their internal use is connected with the warm or hot sulphur baths. I would make the same remark

---

* See Lancet and Observer, Cincinnati, O., for February, 1859.

in reference to *mercurial disease,* commonly so called, or *secondary lues,* often *habitues* of mineral fountains: in such cases we may look to the free internal use of the water, with hot sulphur bathing, with much hope.

Dr. Dawson, in his "Observations at the Springs," has given all the essential directions necessary for the government of invalids in the use of the waters. And as a somewhat long experience in the administration of similar waters enables me to recognize the vast importance to the invalid of attending to such directions, I shall be excused, I hope, for urging their observance upon all who seek to derive the sanative effects of the Ohio White Sulphur. Especially do I commend to all invalid visitors, the very judicious "suggestions" of Dr. Dawson, as to *"the best manner of using the water,"* the *" time for drinking,"* and *"the quantity to be drank."*

CHALYBEATE SPRINGS.

In addition to the Sulphur Artesian fountain of which we have been treating, there are in close proximity to it, and within the Spring Lawn, three other mineral springs deserving of notice. They are all impregnated with *iron*—two of them strongly so. They are known as the *Chalybeate*, the *Magnesian*, and the *Saline Chalybeate* Springs.

It will be seen, by comparing the analyses of the three last-named springs, that their *qualitative* character, in some respects, is essentially the same; the principal difference between them being a larger amount of Sulphate of Magnesia, with a smaller amount of Iron in the *Magnesian* spring, which renders it more purgative, but less tonic than the other two.

Dr. Dawson having noticed these springs in his "Observations," and given the analysis of each, I shall only briefly refer to their therapeutic character as ferruginous waters, offer a few suggestions as to their applicability as remedies, with some directions designed to guide the invalid in their proper administration. I do this with the hope that my suggestions may be useful to those who may not have it in their power to avail themselves of personal medical advice, before entering upon the use of the waters.

The action of chalybeate waters, as is generally known, is tonic, and where there is not an excited, or phlogozed state of the vessels, or a congested condition of the organs that contra-indicate their use, they constitute the most efficient and reliable remedy of the tonic class. While they act primarily upon the stomach, all the other organs and tissues speedily participate in their effects. Their action upon the absorbents and the great capillary system is distinctly marked by the increase of their tone, and consequently an increased force and vigor in the performance of their functions. Hence, in cases of simple atony, or debility, unaccompanied with fever, inflammation, or visceral engorgement, they are found to be certainly and speedily beneficial.

When the system has been exhausted by prior violent disease, that has left no point of irritation that would be readily excited by rapid repletion, or the direct stimulation of remedies, chalybeate waters are found to have a very happy effect.

In the second stages of *Scrofula*, in *Dropsical* effusions, and in *Chronic Intermittents*, they are often employed with good success.

In cases of paucity, or poverty of blood, connected as such cases generally are, with languor, cool skin, and a moist and pale tongue, with feebleness of pulse, chalybeate waters exert the most admirable effects.

Slowness and feebleness, in functional secretions, as well as imperfect sympathetic action between the organs, are readily removed by this remedy; while on the other hand, excessive func-

2

tional action, if attended with inflammation or irritation, will be aggravated by its use. Consequently, when such waters are prescribed to relieve slow, or imperfect digestion, it should be done under the conviction that the impaired function is not dependent upon irritation of the stomach, bowels, or kidneys. The same remark applies to impaired functions of the womb, or any other part of the organism.

Chalybeate waters are found beneficial in the *sequelæ* of long-continued and exhausting discharges, whether of a sanguineous, mucous, or serous character; provided there be no phlogozed condition of the system, nor seat of irritation that might be aggravated by their stimulant effects. These remarks are equally applicable, whether the discharges have been from the course of the alimentary canal, the bladder, or the womb.

For *Fluor Albus*, and for chronic discharges from the urethra, they are found very serviceable.

In *Amenorrhœa*, and its general attendant sterility, chalybeate waters have always borne a high and deserved celebrity; indeed, if they had no other claim to public favor, than their admitted efficacy in such cases, they would still occupy a high place among the most valued remedies.

In addition to the use of chalybeate waters as an independent remedy, I have from long experience at the Virginia White Sulphur, where there is a chalybeate spring, found great advantage in many cases, from the occasional use of it in connection with the regular use of the sulphur water—and the same practice can be pursued at the Ohio White Sulphur, with equal advantage. Indeed, in many cases the use of a chalybeate to follow the alterative effects of sulphur water, is absolutely necessary to perfect a cure.

This is particularly true of *Neuralgia, Gastralgia*, and of that peculiar nervous and debilitated state of the system, which results as a consequence of excessive, or improper indulgences.

METHOD OF ADMINISTRATION, ETC.

With regard to the method of administering chalybeate waters,—they are advantageously taken in doses of from four to six tumblerfuls in the course of the day. Half the quantity used in the twenty-four hours, should be taken in the morning, before breakfast; the remainder on an empty stomach, before dinner and tea. Their good effects ought soon to be perceived, in an improved appetite, and by augmented energy and strength.

Occasionally, such waters are found to oppress the stomach, cause pain in the epigastrium, nausea, colic, with redness of the tongue, heat of the skin, and sometimes diarrhœa. If such symptoms occur, the water should be discontinued, temporarily or permanently, agreeably to the force of the symptoms.

Persons who have an irritable stomach, and especially such as are suffering from a thickening of the coats of the stomach, can not use such waters to advantage.

To be most efficacious, these waters should be used fresh at the spring, as by transportation, even for short distances, they deposit a portion of their salts, and lose that freshness which is essential to their comfortable toleration by the stomach, if not to their medicinal efficacy.

OBSERVATIONS

AT THE

OHIO WHITE SULPHUR SPRINGS,

BY

W. W. DAWSON, M. D., Cincinnati.*

THE medical men of Ohio have long felt the
need of mineral springs near home; of some convenient and meritorious place to which they
could send patients of a certain class; some place
combining a healthy location, agreeable scenery,
suitable provisions both for comfort and recreation, with mineral waters of undoubted virtue.
Attention has often been called, by members of
our profession to the subject,—to the propriety
of investigating the mineral springs within our
own State; but as no provisions, legal or otherwise, have ever been made for analyzing them,
or testing their curative powers, they have been
allowed to rest in obscurity, and physicians who
have had patients that they were well satisfied

* See Cincinnati Lancet and Observer, for February, 1859.

would be most benefited by the use of certain
kinds of medicated waters, have been compelled
to advise these patients to remain at home, and
do without the remedy, rather than undergo the
fatigue consequent upon a journey to some distant watering-place.   Conscious of this great
want, the Ohio State Medical Society, during its
session at Columbus in 1856, appointed a com-
mittee, of which Dr. Wm. Trevitt was chairman,
to "report upon the mineral waters of the State."

In a report which Dr. Trevitt made to the society at its next session, the following judicious
and suggestive remarks are found: "From the
earliest history of civilization, whether under
Christian or heathen dispensation, and long before the light of chemical science had dawned
upon the world, medical springs were known,
appreciated, and thronged by thousands of anxious invalids, in pursuit of health by imbibing
their healing waters, and laving in their luxuri-
ous baths, as well as by votaries of pleasure, who,
in the enjoyment of their own smiles reflected
from the placid waters, found the fountain of
happiness vainly sought by ancient philosophy,
or modern conventional forms of fashionable society.   A long list of names of the most distin-
guished ancients, graced by those of Hippocrates

and Galen, bear testimony to their efficacy; and
Celsus, in his eight books on medicine, assigned
to kind Nature's pharmacy a high position in the
healing art. Our transatlantic brethren, more
particularly those of France and Germany, have
directed their attention very largely to this important subject, the waters of their mineral
springs having been analyzed with great care
and accuracy; and those deemed efficacious, are
thronged with visitors in pursuit of health, under the guidance of the most eminent medical
advisers; many of these springs enjoying a
world-wide reputation in the treatment of
disease."

Of the bequests made to us here in the West
of these health-giving fountains, by the great
Father of all, the report says: "There can be no
reason to doubt but Nature has been as liberal in
the dispensation of her pharmaceutical and medicinal agents, ready prepared from the mineral
kingdom, in this country, and adapted to the
treatment of disease in its protean forms, as she
has been lavish of her favors in other depart-
ments of life; and yet, with the exception of a
few of the States, the analysis of these waters
has been comparatively neglected, or but care-
lessly performed."

Notwithstanding this inexcusable indifference, some of our States have demonstrated the fact, that they possess within their borders, springs of marked medicinal qualities, and equal, perhaps, to those found in any part of Europe. The experience of the last few years, but more especially the observations of the past season, show conclusively that in this respect Ohio is not deficient; that the "OHIO WHITE SULPHUR SPRINGS" are entitled to a high position among first-class mineral waters. The remedial virtues of these waters have long been known by those residing in their immediate vicinity; but, through the liberality of the present proprietor, Andrew Wilson, Esq., they have, within the past year, been analyzed and brought into general notice.

Having spent some three months of the summer at these springs, and having had somewhat liberal opportunities for studying the effect of their waters upon various forms of disease, as quite a considerable proportion of the large number who resorted to them, during that period, were health-seeking invalids, we have concluded that it would be but a just tribute to the merits of the place, and at the same time serviceable to the public, to lay the result of our observations before the profession. These observations fully indorse the high estimate which learned men, in all ages, have placed upon these "fountains of health." In Europe, as before suggested, physicians of decided ability, are located at the spas, whose duty it is to apply the waters to disease, watch their influence, analyze their virtues, and determine carefully their value as medicinal agents,—thus obtaining much reliable and valuable information. But in this country such judiciousness has not been observed, except in comparatively few instances.

As the principal of these exceptions, however, the White Sulphur Springs of Virginia may be mentioned. For more than twenty years, Dr. J. J. Moorman, a learned man in his profession, has been administering this water in disease, and carefully observing and recording its effects. These observations this gentleman has published in a volume of some three hundred pages,—a work which may be read with very great advantage by both the professional and the non-professional reader. It is an agreeable book, written in a pleasing and unpretending style; but its chief merit is, that it abounds in well digested facts, making an important contribution to our, in this respect, deficient literature.

3

Upon the estate there are five springs, four of
which have decided medicinal properties; the
fifth is remarkable for the purity of its waters.
They, from their chemical characteristics, have
been named respectively. *The White Sulphur
Spring, The Chalybeate Spring, The Magnesian
Spring, The Saline Chalybeate Spring,* and *The Pure
Water Spring.*

These springs have been analyzed, during the
past summer, by Prof. E. S. Wayne, the result
of which will be seen as we progress.

The springs are situated upon the west bank of
the Scioto, near the southern border of Delaware
county. The Scioto here presents features so entirely different from those characterizing it in its
course from Columbus to the Ohio river, that it
would be hardly recognized as the same stream.
For some distance above and below the springs
its current is rapid, its banks being bluff and
rocky; having, in making its way from the higher
lands farther north, cut its channel through a
heavy limestone, fragments of which are every
where strewn along its bed.

The country surrounding the springs is situated upon the southern slope of Ohio, some distance from the summit level.

The springs are nearly six hundred feet above the Ohio river at Cincinnati, and about one thousand feet higher than the ocean. This elevation, taken in connection with the fact that the rock is every where either at or near the surface, and that the land is beautifully undulated, renders the locality as free from malarious influence as a mountain region.

Geological Position.—The Scioto, as we have before said, here cuts its way through what is known as cliff limestone—so called from its heavy, massive structure. This formation is present at Dayton, Eaton, Springfield, Hillsboro' and Columbus. It appears above the blue limestone, half way between Cincinnati and the springs, and continues at the surface until it is lost beneath the shales and sandstones some distance farther east and north-east. The cliff limestone, from which these waters issue, is below and hence it is geologically older than the coal series. Although solid, and non-porous in its organization generally, it here abounds in large cavities, as is shown by the existence in the vicinity of numerous conical depressions, known

usually as "sink holes," which receive and carry
off large quantities of water. Through one of
these cavities, at the depth of one hundred and
sixty feet, flows the remarkable stream of sulphur
water from which the principal spring is supplied. When, some thirty years ago, an individual, who was boring for salt, struck this vein,
the water at once arose to the surface, and has
ever since flowed with unabated force: the
changes of seasons, or of temperature producing
no effect whatever, either upon the quantity of
water, or the force with which it is ejected. It
is now, by its own momentum, thrown up the
hill about one hundred yards, to a beautiful marble receiver.

It is a curious, and at the same time an extremely interesting fact, that in geological position the Ohio White Sulphur Springs correspond
with some of the most celebrated mineral springs
in the world. As an instance of this suggestive
correspondence, we may refer to the celebrated
White Sulphur Springs in Virginia. These, like
the Ohio White Sulphur, issue from the great
Devonian formation, the situation of which is
immediately below the coal-bearing series. This
interesting correspondence in position, and in the
character of the stratæ from which these waters

are given, was noticed by Dr. S. P. Hildreth, in 1837, when that gentleman was connected with the geological survey of this State. In that part of his report made to the legislature, which he devotes to the "Ohio Salines," in referring to those found in Delaware county, he says: "These springs appear to rise in a similar formation to those of Greenbrier valley, in Virginia: viz., a carboniferous limestone. There, several weak muriate of soda springs are found by boring; but these deposits are more celebrated for their sulphur springs, than for those of salt water."

The cliff limestone, so rich in all its resources as to give these five sparkling streams, all differing essentially, here rests upon the first of the fossiliferous rocks—the superior layers of the great Silurian system, which, under the name of Blue Limestone, is found underlying all other formations, from the Gulf of Mexico to Lake Erie, being continuous and characteristic throughout the entire extent.

THE WHITE SULPHUR SPRING.

Of the five springs the White Sulphur may be ranked of first importance, from its adaptation to a wider range of disease. ·

Temperature, 52° Fahrenheit.

Prof. E. S. Wayne found the following substances present in the water:

GASES, { Sulphureted Hydrogen,
        { Carbonic acid.

Chloride of magnesium.	Oxide of iron.
Chloride of sodium.	Carbonate of lime.
Chloride of calcium.	Sulphuret of calcium.
Sulphate of magnesia.	Iodine.
Sulphate of lime.	Traces of organic matter.

This, like most mineral waters, is essentially
alterative in its action; but it differs widely in
its mode of operating with the ordinary drugs of
that class. With the salts which it contains held
in a state of high dilution, it enters the system,
and, coming into contact with the sentient
mouths of the absorbents, is carried to the blood-
vessels, and then by means of the circulation to
every tissue of the body. Upon this subject Prof.
John Bell, in his work on "Mineral Springs,"
says: "In reference to the secondary and remote,
and avowedly salutary effects of mineral waters,
when we reflect on the large mucous surface of
the entire digestive canal, to every portion of
which they are applied, and by which they are
freely absorbed, thus reaching all the tissues of
the animal frame, and bearing in mind, also, the
number and variety of the ingredients which
enter into their composition, we are prepared to

echo the language of a French writer* on the
subject, when he says: 'In general, mineral
waters revive the languishing circulation, give a
new direction to the vital energies, re-establish
the perspiratory action of the skin, bring back to
their physiological type the vitiated or suppressed
secretions, provoke salutary evacuations, either
by urine or stool, or by transpiration: they bring
about an intimate transmutation, a profound
change in the organism; they saturate the sick
body, to make use of the energetic expression of
a modern author. How many persons, aban-
doned by their physicians, have found health at
mineral springs! How many individuals, exhausted by violent disease, have recovered, by a
journey to mineral springs, their tone, ready
movements and energy, to restore which attempts
in other ways might have been made with less
certainty of success.'" Dr. Gairdner, in dis-
cussing the *modus operandi* of mineral waters,
says: "The simple circumstance of dilution will
certainly facilitate the operation of matters
which might otherwise pass little changed
through the alimentary canal; and from the
extremely minute state of division in which the
active particles are presented to the sentient

* Pateissier, Sur les Eaux Minerales.

mouths of the capillary absorbents, it is more
than probable that they are directly absorbed
into the circulating mass."

Regarding this water, then, as decidedly *alterative*, the range of diseases in which it is applicable will be apparent: such, for instance, as
chronic affections of the stomach, liver, kidneys,
bowels, skin, etc. Upon the functions of these
important organs it exerts a marked influence—
stimulating those which are inactive, and restoring a healthy secretion in such as have departed
from a normal condition.

DISEASES TREATED BY THE WHITE SULPHUR WATER.

We trust that a frank history of our experience in the application of this remedy to disease
may tend to direct the attention of our profession
to the investigations of the mineral waters of the
West. As before said, the medical men of Europe, and in some localities of the eastern portion of our own country, have studied these
agents with great care: they look upon them as
important adjuvants to the resources of our art,
and are using them with decided advantage in
the treatment of many of the ills to which
humanity is subject.

Diseases of the Stomach.—These disorders are

numerous, and many of them of a grave character, giving the physician in their treatment much trouble and anxiety; and often, while they do not immediately jeopardize life, yet completely baffle all his efforts for a radical and permanent cure.

Dyspepsia.—At the head of these gastric disorders stands dyspepsia, with all its protean forms and varied complications. As persons laboring under this affection are always among the *habitues* of watering places, several well marked cases came under our control, and were treated by this water alone, and with a success, too, which warrants high hopes of its capabilities in disorders of the stomach generally. One of the first indications of a salutary change in these cases was the removal of the constipation, so often a concomitant, if not the cause, of dyspepsia, and which under ordinary circumstances it is so difficult to reach successfully with drugs. Following this was a gradual restoration of the healthy functions of the stomach; the cardialgia, flatulence, acidity, uneasiness and pain after eating, disappeared, one by one, and the appetite finally became normal. A very severe case of dyspepsia, complicated with serious derangement of the nervous system, was presented for treatment; it was of long standing, and had been subjected to various modes of medication without benefit. This case, as will appear, shows the absolute necessity of using the water judiciously, in reference to *the time of drinking it, the quantity to be drank, and the length of time it should be continued.* The gentleman affected, for some weeks after his arrival, consumed the water in large quantities, and at irregular periods—at morning, noon, night, and at the intermediate hours. For the first week he had felt better; his liver being aroused, his bowels freely moved, his kidneys stimulated to increased action. But by this over indulgence he had brought on a disturbance, such as might be expected to follow the excessive use of remedies of this class. He was advised to discontinue the water for a few days, and, on resuming it, to drink but some four or five glasses before breakfast, allowing himself a half-hour's gentle exercise, such as walking, between each draught. Under this course his improvement was rapid, giving him every earnest of a permanent cure. But before the remedy had had time to produce its entire effect, matters of business called him imperatively home. This was a matter to be regretted, for his condition was one well calculated to try the real powers of the water, not only upon the stomach, but in giving tone to a broken-down nervous system.

Inaction of the Stomach.—There are many cases of disorder of the stomach where, without positive, or at least apparent disease, there is, if we may be allowed the expression, a mere indisposition to digestion, a want of power, to some extent, in the stomach to perform its functions. The food, after eating, does not become acid, but remains in the stomach for a time unchanged, producing a sensation of uneasiness, rather than pain : if eructation occurs, the food tastes as sweet as it did before it was swallowed. Associated with these symptoms is generally found an indifferent appetite. In this condition, the water had a most gratifying effect ; under its influence the appetite in a few days became regulated, and the stomach was aroused from its passive state to one of normal activity.

Acidity of the Stomach.—Among gastric lesions, not amounting to gastritis, or well marked dyspepsia, we often find persistent acidity of the stomach. This acidity does not follow every meal,—sometimes it is felt but once during the day, and again it may not occur more than three or four times through the week. As a general thing, this condition is the forerunner of more

serious disturbance; but in one case which came
under my observation during the season, it had
continued for some eight or ten years. The
person in whom it occurred remained at
the springs until it had entirely disappeared.
We saw him also in December, and up to that
time he had had no symptom of its return.

The foregoing will be sufficient to indicate to
the profession the applicability of this water to
many of the more grave disorders to which the
stomach is subject.

Diseases of the Liver.—Decidedly marked, also,
is the influence of this water in diseases of this
organ ; and, indeed, as heretofore suggested, in
many of the affections of the chylopoietic viscera.
Prominent among them, in consequence of its
size, importance of function, and its singular li-
ability to disease, stands the liver. In some of
the lesions of this gland sulphur water has long
been held in deservedly high estimation. The
following remarks on the action of the White
Sulphur Water of Virginia, by Dr. Moorman, agrees well with our observation in the use
of this : "The *modus operandi* of sulphur water
upon this viscus is dissimilar, we conceive, from
that of mercury, yet the effects of the two agents
are strikingly analogous. The potent and con-

trolling influences of the water over the secre-
tory functions of the liver must be regarded as a
specific quality of the agent, and as constituting
an important therapeutical feature in the value
of the article for diseases of this organ. Its influence upon this gland is gradually but surely
to unload it when engorged, and to stimulate it
to a healthy exercise of its function when torpid.
The control which it may be made to exercise
over the liver in correcting and restoring its energies is often as astonishing as it is gratifying, es-
tablishing a copious flow of healthy bile, a consequent activity of the bowels, imparting vigor to
the whole digestive and assimilative functions,
and consequently energy and strength to the
body, and life and elasticity to the spirit."

Subjected to treatment were cases of chronic
inflammation of the liver, of inaction, of engorgement, and of congestion ; and although relief was
not found in all instances, yet such was the per-
centage of positive cures in some, and partial in
others, that we feel safe in recommending this
water to the profession as a remedy worthy of all
confidence in many of the more severe forms of
biliary disease.

Diseases of the Bowels.—This remedy seemed
to have some peculiar power in rectifying disor-

ders of the bowels, possessing certainly a poten-
cy in this respect seldom elsewhere seen. Such
a case as the following will illustrate what is
meant. An old gentleman arrived at the springs
in a condition calculated to draw largely upon
one's sympathies. For several years he had suf-
fered with dyspepsia of very grave character.
Prominent among the symptoms was an obstinate constipation, which had resisted all treatment. Under this his system flagged, the secretions had become vitiated; emaciation followed,
accompanied by effusions into the cellular tissue
and into the serous sacs of the chest. The effusions soon assumed a serious aspect, and became
so troublesome as to make respiration painfully
laborious. To keep at all comfortable he was
compelled to resort, almost daily, to large doses
of the most drastic cathartics, to reduce the accu-
mulations of water, so as to render his breathing
endurable. In his own language, he had had " to
live on nauseous medicines." In this apparently
hopeless condition he arrived at the springs. He
did not expect to be cured ; but his great desire
was, to be made comparatively comfortable, and
to avoid, if possible, the use of drugs. After
drinking the water for a few days with caution,
there were evident indications of improvement,

which soon became decided : it seemed to be admirably adapted to his case, acting promptly and kindly upon him in every respect, and in time it imparted somewhat of tone and vigor to his system,—it *corrected that obstinate constipation*, that had resisted the influence of all drugs ; it stimulated the kidneys from a scanty to a free and copious discharge of healthy urine ; and arrested, for the time he was at the springs at least, the pleuritic and pericardiac effusions. It need hardly be here remarked, that the history of such a case as the above will do more to inspire the profession with confidence in the *positive* medical virtues of this water than the most ingenious speculations that could be made, or the most plausible theories that could be suggested by the most fertile brain.

The remedy was no less promising, so far as our limited opportunities enabled us to observe, in hemorrhoids, cholera infantum, chronic diarrhœa, etc. Two cases of that painful and troublesome disease, hemorrhoids, were treated by the remedy with advantage. Constipation, the most aggravating and the almost constant attendant upon piles, was soon relieved ; and, no sooner was relief apparent in this respect, than the disease manifested marked improvement. The water, by equalizing the circulation, by rectifying the congested state of the capillaries, produced a salutary change in the rectum.

Affections of the Kidneys.—In these the sulphur water should be prescribed with very great caution; for while its influence in some will be decidedly beneficial, in others, by directly stimulating the kidneys, it will do much injury. Of this latter class may be mentioned Albuminuria and Bright's disease. A gentleman, who had been unadvisedly using this water, had an already large amount of albumen in his urine sensibly increased. He was, after his case had been diagnosed, induced to relinquish the use of the sulphur water, and resort to the chalybeate spring. He remained at the springs some two or three weeks, during which time the albuminous secretion had been diminished very greatly. But in chronic inflammation of the kidneys, and in defective secretion, other than that already mentioned, the sulphur water may be prescribed confidently.

In one case of deficient and vitiated secretion, dependent upon disorder of the stomach, and a consequent want of proper assimilation, the powers of the agent were in a few days apparent, changing both the quality and quantity of the urine.

Chronic Inflammations.—What we have said of the applicability of this water in chronic hepatitis, nephritis, etc., may be affirmed of most chronic inflammations; such, for instance, as that condition of the mucous membrane of the bowels found in diarrhœa of long standing; that engorgement of the spleen in old cases of ague; that affection of the synovial surfaces of the joints in persistent rheumatism. The modes by which these lesions are removed are to some extent obscure, like similar questions arising from the action of many of our remedies; but this much we may affirm, that it stimulates the vessels, supplies deficiencies in the salts of the fluids, absorption is promoted, and the functions of secretion and excretion are brought to a healthy standard.

One severe case of *chronic pericarditis*, associated with pain and a sense of weakness in the region of the kidneys, was successfully treated during the summer. The person afflicted was nineteen years of age, had been reared in the country, and a general debility showed that his entire system was sympathizing with the difficulty about the heart; which, being of long standing, and having proved invulnerable to all remedies, both he and his friends had well-nigh ceased to hope

4

for relief.   He drank some four or five glasses of the water every morning, and applied it to the surface in the form of warm sulphur baths.   After remaining under this treatment for two months, all traces of the affection had disappeared, and he left the springs changed from a weak and feeble condition to one of robust health.

Diseases of the Lungs.—In these the sulphur water should be used with some care, and not until the case is satisfactorily diagnosed; for, while it is well adapted to some, in others its tendency will be pernicious.   In congestion of the lungs, however, and of the bronchial tubes, where there is no excitement, it may be prescribed with good effect.   Chest affections, depending on perverted nutrition, like the following case, may be improved, and the disease often held in check, if not cured.   In this case there were great emaciation, pain in the left side of long standing, occasional attacks of hæmoptysis, associated with a derangement of the stomach amounting to well defined dyspepsia.   The improvement of the patient, who had an extremely delicate physique, will be sufficiently manifest by the fact, that under the influence of the water some fifteen pounds were gained in about twelve weeks.

Tubercular Consumption.—The water in this disease, when once fully developed, does not promise well ; and the same may be said of scrofulous diseases generally.

Cutaneous Affections.—The well established reputation of sulphur waters in these affections, and its direct tendency to and its stimulating effect upon the skin, would augur favorably of this water in surface disorders ; but no well marked case continued its use long enough to thoroughly test its remedial properties.

Chlorosis.—A very serious case of this was brought to the springs, and in some eight weeks its morbid paleness, sharpness of feature, nervousness, palpitation and breathlessness, had given place to rotundity of form, cheerfulness of mind, vigor of body and a rosy-hued complexion. We may be enabled to explain such effects by looking to the efficacy of the agent in re-establishing the broken-down functions of nutrition, as well as by the iron found in its composition ; but, as a general thing, such anæmic conditions were most benefited by another spring—the *Chalybeate.*

Rheumatism.—The sulphur water is highly esteemed by those who have resorted to it in earlier years for rheumatism ; but the past summer

furnished little by which its virtues in this respect could be computed. But applied in the
form of hot, warm, and steam sulphur baths, with
its internal use, we have no doubt but that it
will sustain the reputation which such waters
have long had in rheumatic and gouty affections.

Dropsies.—In speaking of the effect of the water upon diseases of the bowels, we referred to a
case in which, under its use, effusions within the
serous cavities of the chest were arrested.
Some salutary changes were effected, also, in the
only case of ascites which was at the springs
during our stay; but the subject of it only remained a week—a length of time not sufficient
in which to receive any permanent advantage.

THE WATER WITHOUT ITS GASES.

There were cases observed during the season
that were the most benefited by the water after
being deprived of its gases. Fresh from the
spring, in these instances, its influence was not
salutary: the tongue became slightly furred,
thirst unusual manifested itself, together with a
sense of fulness about the head,—showing that
the agent used was of too stimulating character.
But in these cases it was gratifying to find that,
from drinking the water after it had been stand-

ing long enough to lose its gaseous properties, none of these unpleasant symptoms presented themselves. The non-gaseous water acted kindly, and in time produced effects peculiar to it when taken fresh from the fountain. To this course we were led by having before us the twenty years' observation of the venerable Dr. Moorman, who, in his work, devotes a chapter to the discussion of the "Relative Virtues of the Saline and Gaseous Contents of the White Sulphur Water." In that chapter he shows that a judicious discrimination is essentially necessary in this respect; that while most persons may take the water as it flows fresh from the spring, others should not drink it until after its gases have had time to escape.

SOME SUGGESTIONS AS TO BEST MANNER OF USING THE SULPHUR WATER.

It would be well for all who visit the spas to remember that mineral waters, whether pleasant or unpleasant to the taste, are medicines, and as such should be treated. No rational person, who wants the effect of a certain drug, would take it at all times, under all circumstances, or whenever he happened to be near it; nor would he go upon the principle that the more taken the better. but he would take it according to some specific rule, and with both caution and fidelity. *This is not more true of ordinary drugs than it is of mineral waters.* Yet there were many persons who resorted to the springs for the benefit of the water, who drank it without thought or system, *in large quantities—in small quantities, at any* and *all hours*—before and after meals—on getting up in the morning, and on going to bed at night; and among those who used it in this reckless manner, not a single person is remembered who was essentially and permanently benefited. This, like mineral waters of its class, is an extremely delicate agent, and requires much cautiousness in its application, that the system may be kept *delicately sensitive* to its influence; an excessive use of such agents blunts this susceptibility, and renders them inert.

To illustrate what is meant, we may remark, that those persons who drank large quantities were at first gratified with its purgative effects; but, on continuing its use at all hours of the day, they were soon disappointed even in this respect; while those who used it in small quantities, but irregularly also, were equally disappointed because it did not produce at once some extraordinary change or constitutional revolution. On the contrary, those who drank the water judiciously, and thus kept their systems sensitive to its impression, were always gratified with the result.

It will be at once apparent, that in prescribing such a remedy, no definite rules can be given: we may suggest some general directions, yet modifications must be made to suit special cases, in reference to—

The time of drinking,
The quantity to be drank,—and
The length of time its use should be continued.

The Time of Drinking.—In the large majority of cases the water was used principally before the fast of the morning was broken. The propriety of resorting to the spring thus early will be readily appreciated—the stomach is empty, and having had the long rest of the night, it will be in better condition to receive and appropriate the remedy at this, than at any other time. A couple of glasses were usually directed to be taken before dinner—say at 12 M., if the person dined at two, and breakfasted at seven or eight o'clock, thus allowing sufficient time for the complete digestion of the morning meal. In a case of dyspepsia, the water was used at meals alone, and with the happiest result; it seemed to agree best with the patient taken in this manner. But as a general rule the plan of using it at meals, with invalids especially, was not advantageous. Upon this subject Dr. Moorman says: "Now and then advantage is derived from using the water at meals, and sometimes a tolerance is established for it in this way which can not be achieved by any other." To persons in health at the springs these precautions, of course, are not necessary; becoming very fond of the water, they often relish it keenly while eating, and, what is very remarkable, with some it supersedes, for the time being at least, their taste for coffee and tea. Could it destroy permanently the desire for these two questionable beverages, with many it "would be a consummation devoutly to be wished."

The following remarks from the work of Prof. John Bell, on "Mineral Springs," forcibly illustrate the propriety of a careful selection of the hours at which to use mineral waters: "An invalid may drink a moderate quantity of the water before breakfast with comfort and advantage, but not be able to do the same before dinner with equally good effects. He may be able to take the water both before breakfast and dinner, and yet if he drink in the evening he will perhaps have a restless night, and be worse next morning than he had been twenty-four hours before."

No very definite rule could be laid down for the government of the patient in this respect: the efficient quantity depending upon the person, habits, age, sex, character of disease, etc. A gentleman, who was afflicted with congestion of the liver, accompanied by constipation and indigestion, was directed to use four or five glasses before breakfast, with an interval of twenty to thirty minutes between each glass. Under this quantity, in about two weeks his bowels became regular, his appetite good, and the clear hue imparted to his skin indicated the relief which had been given to the liver. There were some who took not more than two glasses before breakfast, and the same number before dinner, with marked benefit. Again, there were others who required from six to ten glasses during the day to produce the full alterative effects requisite to a cure.

One of the most reliable indications for moderating the quantity was an undue secretion of urine; an alterative action being generally obtained by an amount which, while it increased

5

the discharge of urine, did not stimulate the kidneys to an unhealthy activity. Dr. Moorman, from whose work we have so liberally quoted, gives the history of a case full of instruction upon this point. It was that of a gentleman who had been under treatment for a "complicated stomach and neuralgic affection," and "had used the water twelve days, in small doses, with happy effect." "I did not see him," says Dr. M., "for two or three days, and then casually met him. I was astonished to find him greatly changed for the worse. His appetite, before good, had almost entirely ceased; his system was irritable and feverish; could not sleep at night; and in every respect was sensibly worse: had begun to despair, and proposed leaving for home, as he was 'satisfied the water was not agreeing with him.' I accused him of impropriety in diet, or of other imprudences; but he satisfied me that he had followed my directions in all 'such things,'—but he had so far varied from my advice in the use of the water as to take *sixteen*, instead of *six* glasses daily, for the last few days. I advised this gentleman, as I would all others who have committed a similar 'debauch' on cold water, to discontinue its use entirely for a time—take some opening medicines, and then return to the use of it in rational doses. This plan was pursued by him, and with the happiest results." A case somewhat like the above, came under our notice during the season, reference to which is made under the head of diseases of the stomach. The subject of it was afflicted with a grave disorder, involving both the stomach and nervous system, and for some two weeks after arriving at the springs he drank the water in large quantities, and at irregular periods. At the end of this time, we found him fast growing out of conceit of the remedy. He had come to the conclusion that, instead of benefiting him, it had produced more or less excitement, and had made him restless. He was advised to lessen the quantity, and take what he did at definite hours. As long as he pursued this course he gained relief, and had an earnest of a permanent cure.

The only way, however, to determine the efficient quantity is by intelligently noting its effects, by studying critically the case under its influence; by beginning thus cautiously, a few days enabled us to determine the matter. Again, the quantity will depend upon the effect to be produced; more being required to produce purgation than to promote an alterative action; less was necessary to act upon the kidneys than to stimulate the skin;

and although a few small doses daily, were found efficacious in chronic diarrhœa, yet large and frequent draughts were essential in some of the disorders of long standing.

LENGTH OF TIME THE WATER SHOULD BE USED.

The length of time which patients, to whom this water promises well, should continue under its influence, must of necessity vary greatly. Some were cured in *four weeks;* others were compelled to use it for *two months* before being restored to health; others obtained the same result in six weeks—and there were those who, afflicted with mild forms of disease, obtained the full effect of the remedy in two weeks. What we ordinarily call functional diseases were often promptly relieved in a few days.

SULPHUR BATHS.

The utility of baths in many forms of disease is well understood; but we think we may claim for sulphur water more than ordinary excellence in this respect—when applied in the form of *warm* or *hot baths* its influence upon the skin being well marked, and well defined. The reputation of such waters in diseases of the skin proper has long been established; but in this connection we desire to direct attention, more particularly, to the action of this water upon the skin, where it is suffering from a disorder of some of the principal organs of the body; such as its dry, scabrous state, found in duodenal dyspepsia; or that husky, sallow complexion belonging to chronic hepatitis; or that passive state of its capillaries in dropsy; or that inactive condition left by the more grave forms of fever. Upon the skin, under such circumstances, the influence of the sulphur baths was singularly satisfactory, imparting tone to the entire surface, stimulating its vessels, bringing back its wonted softness, and re-establishing its natural hue. The influence of such changes in this important tissue, in the treatment of diseases, need not here be insisted upon.

THE CHALYBEATE SPRING.

The water of this spring is beautifully clear and sparkling.

Temperature, 56° Fahrenheit.

The analysis shows it to contain *iron* in two forms: viz.—

Sulphate of Iron,	Oxide of Iron.

It also contains—

Carbonic acid gas,	Carbonate of lime,
Sulphate of magnesia,	Potassa,
Chloride of calcium,	Sulphate of lime,
Iodine,	Traces of organic matter.

This water, like all of its class, is essentially tonic, and as such was used in cases of debility, anæmia, etc., with advantage. As an adjuvant to the sulphur it is of first importance. In several patients treated principally by the latter, there was great benefit derived from the bracing, invigorating influence of the chalybeate. Some cases, after having had an alterative effect produced by the white sulphur, were placed upon the chalybeate for the completion of the cure. Thus draughting upon two different waters in the treatment of certain forms of disease is a frequent custom in Germany, where a person, after remaining under the influence of an alterative water until his disordered and vitiated secretions are corrected, is sent to some distant spring, which, by its tonic powers, may invigorate his enfeebled system. Here such change may be made when necessary without much trouble, as the two springs of opposite qualities are upon the same estate, and distant from each other but a few hundred yards.

Our opportunities for studying the effects of the chalybeate water, when employed by itself, were limited to a few cases; hence, most of what we shall say of it will be merely suggestive. But, limited as were our observations, they were yet sufficient to justify us in recommending this to the profession as a first-class spring of the kind. The iron here is in better association than is usually seen in this country; for in most places where limestone abounds—and it is almost every where throughout the West—the carbonate of lime found in chalybeate waters is so great as to render them as remedial agents completely worthless, if not positively hurtful.

As an independent remedy, by imparting its iron and its various salts to the impoverished blood, it will be found peculiarly adapted to many of the diseases seen every year at watering-places; such as anæmic conditions, chlorosis, the early stages of scrofula, amenorrhœa, dysmenorrhœa, some of the lesions of the kidneys, etc.

The gentleman heretofore spoken of, whose urine contained a large amount of albumen, and who was also suffering with a very severe sympathetic affection of the lungs—so severe, indeed, that it had been looked upon as the original disease—derived great benefit from this water. After resorting to this spring for two weeks, the secretion of albumen was diminished one-half. A person afflicted with scrofulous disease, while resorting to this spring, increased in weight some fifteen pounds.

THE MAGNESIAN SPRING.

The water of this spring has a bitterish taste, resembling a dilute solution of Epsom salts.

Temperature, 54° Fahrenheit.

The analysis shows that with the

Sulphate of Magnesia

the following substances are associated :

Chloride of calcium,	Carbonate of lime,
Oxide of iron,	Iodine, small,
Sulphate of lime,	Potassa, small,
Earthy phosphates,	Traces of organic matter,

Carbonic acid gas.

This spring, it will be observed, resembles in its composition some of those that have long been esteemed for their remedial virtues; but as an aperient only did we use it, and of its powers farther we can not speak. In this respect—that is, as a laxative—we employed it in some cases in connection with the White Sulphur, and in others it was associated with the Chalybeate. The evacuations produced by it were of good consistence, not watery like those following generally the use of saline cathartics.

The existence here of these three springs, the

White Sulphur, the *Chalybeate*, and the *Magnesian*, forms a combination of much promise; they will enable the physician to adopt either an evacuating, tonic, or alterative plan of treatment. He may, in cases of great debility, combine the tonic and alterative; or in an opposite condition, where there is too much excitement, he may replace the tonic by the aperient; and again, where he is using the Chalybeate, he may require the laxative influence of the Magnesian. Dr. James Johnson, in his "Pilgrimage to the Spas, in pursuit of Health and Recreation," thus refers to a similar association of remedies: "It is often found to be beneficial to combine tonics, alteratives, and aperients in the same formula or prescription, in order that the three indications alluded to may be simultaneously accomplished. It is undeniable, that some of the spas contain within themselves this combination of chalybeates, aperients and alteratives, either of which ingredients can be increased at pleasure on the spot."

THE SALINE CHALYBEATE SPRING.

Temperature, 55° Fahrenheit.

This spring, during the past season, was not resorted to, as it had not been improved, or brought into notice. It was, however, analyzed in November last, by Prof. Wayne, and found to contain—

Sulphate of Lime,	Oxide of Iron,
Sulphate of Magnesia,	Carbonate of Lime,
Chloride of Calcium.	Traces of Potash,

Traces of Organic Matter.

It will be seen by comparison that these springs resemble, in their composition—in the salts and gases which they contain—the far-famed Bedford Springs. At that celebrated watering-place, as here, there is a Sulphur, a Chalybeate, and a Saline Chalybeate.

THE PURE-WATER SPRING.

The remarkable purity of this water, although issuing from beneath a ledge of limestone, gives it claim to a passing notice here. The analysis, by Prof. Wayne, shows it to possess but a trifle, if any, more solid matter than is found in the water of the Ohio river.

POSITIVE CURATIVE VIRTUES OF MINERAL WATERS.

It is said by the incredulous, and more especially by those who have had no experience in their use, and those also who have neglected the literature of mineral springs (confessedly light in this country, but full and reliable in many of the States of Europe), that the recoveries which occur at the spas are more to be attributed to fresh air, change of scenes, genial society, etc., than to any independent remedial virtues in the waters. Now, although much good may and does result from such surroundings—and they are, without doubt, in many instances important adjuvants—yet it is certainly demonstrable, that these waters possess curative powers over and above such circumstances; that these powers produce effects direct and positive, and that many cases are cured by them alone, without any such extraneous aids.

There are, among those who have been benefited by resorting to springs, many who have had, when at home, all the advantages arising from cheerful company, beautiful scenery, and fresh air. There are those also who, instead of being amused and kept cheerful, are gloomy and low-spirited, while using the water—or, at least, until they perceive that it is benefiting them; and, again, there are those who come from rural districts, from salubrious localities, and who have been surrounded with all the comforts of a pleasant country residence. The same may be said of its decided effects with persons confined to their rooms, which are often small and illy ventilated,—of merchants, who are restless, irritable

and anxious, on account of being away from their
business affairs—and of the despairing hypo-
chondriac, who, "despondent, dejected, misan-
thropic, and fidgety," is ever tormenting himself
with hopeless imaginings, and gloomy forebod-
ings.   When these waters exert a salutary influence upon such as the foregoing, we may, without
hypothesis, conclude that they are potent agents,
and that they possess, *per se*, efficient power for
the eradication of diseases of grave character.
Of mineral waters as curative agents, Dr. S.
Hanbury Smith, a gentleman who has had
extensive experience, and who is therefore quali-
fied to estimate them properly, in his work on
"Medicinal Mineral Waters, Natural and Arti-
ficial," writes thus: "That *there is a large series
of chronic diseases, and anomalous disordered conditions, best cured by the use of mineral waters, and
a similar series often incurable by any other known
means*, is a postulate which will undoubtedly be
granted by every practitioner of reputation
throughout the whole continent of Europe.
That, moreover, in *another series of cases, mineral
waters efficiently aid ordinary therapeutic measures*,
and that *in a fourth the effects produced by their
employment afford a valuable source of diagnosis*,
will be as readily granted.   The well established

facts, the long catalogue of observations recorded
by competent observers, leave no room for dis-
pute or cavil about the truth of these proposi-
tions. After all, there is nothing more wonderful
in the curative powers of the compound medicine
called a *mineral water*, in those cases in which it
is specially indicated, than there is in the admitted virtues of the time-tested compounds of the
pharmacopœia, when similarly administered.
Carlsbad water is as much the best medicine in
some cases, as sulphate of quinine is in others;
when all our ordinary chalybeates fail, the administration of the same, or even a much smaller
dose of iron, in some such combination as is
afforded by Pyrmont or the Ferdinands-quelle
of Marienbad, shall gladden us with its happy
effects. In fact, in mineral waters Nature has
presented us with an extensive range of *præpa-
rata et composita*, containing the same ingredients
that we are daily prescribing, only compounded
according to formulæ of her own." Upon the
same subject, Dr. Bell has said: "Nor do we
find the cure of many diseases at watering-places,
by drinking the waters, confined to those who
have left the crowded city and its unwholesome
air. The inhabitants of the country are often
equally benefited by the same course of treat-

ment, although they can not be said to enjoy the additional advantages of change of air, and of rural scenes obtained by the other class.   .   .   .

On the other hand, the dull, unlettered clown, or the exacting logician and mathematician, will often come away cured of their dyspepsia, torpid liver, rheumatism, or long-endured cutaneous disease, to whom society would be more irksome than agreeable." "Animals, moreover," remarks our author, "have been evidently cured of obstinate maladies by this means, without our being able to divide the credit of the cure with country air, change of food, and pleasant company." The interesting case of disease of the serous envelop of the heart, mention of which is made under the head of Chronic Inflammations, is peculiarly significant in this connection, as illustrating forcibly the inherent remedial powers of the sulphur water. The young man affected had been reared in the country, in a healthy region, and the change of his rural to that of spring life was far from being agreeable; he was diffident, lonely, avoided society, and it was only by the constant exertion of his friends that he was kept at the springs; and even after the water had made a favorable impression upon his illness, he insisted upon returning home—and, in fact, until

the completion of his cure, he remained in the
same dissatisfied and cheerless condition. Important as are heartsome associations, a con-
tented, and especially an agreeably occupied
mind, in any plan of treatment, and much as
such a mental state unquestionably facilitates in
many instances the cure, yet here was a complete
recovery from a severe and complicated illness,
effected by the water alone, without any of these
important adjuvants.

MEDICATION DURING THE USE OF THE WATER.

In many instances it was found best to antici-
pate the use of the water by a simple cathartic,
and there were some cases in which obstructions
existed, which had to be removed before the
water could have its entire effects. Connected
with a chronic inflammation was found a well-
marked intermittent fever—this, of course, had
to be treated by the usual remedy, and entirely
removed, before the water could reach the original lesion.

Upon this subject, Dr. James Johnson, from
whom we before quoted, says: "Thilenius, contrary to the custom of most of the spa doctors,
admits that, although the waters alone cure
many disorders, yet in a great many cases appro-

priate medicines are absolutely necessary. He contends however, and I believe with justice, that *many diseases give way to the combination of the waters and medicines, which resist the latter, if unaided by the former.*"

Before concluding our paper, we can not refrain from offering a few suggestions to a class of persons who, although not strictly invalids, yet need annually the influence of such waters.

It may be laid down as a general rule, that all business men, of close, laborious habits, and especially those whose pursuits confine them within doors, have more or less disorder of the liver, and of the digestive organs generally. Each succeeding season of labor renders the recuperative powers of the system more and more feeble, until at last, without something is done to prevent the effect of these annual draughts upon vitality, what was mere disorder assumes the form of positive disease. To such, waters of this kind are peculiarly adapted, and from their judicious use more real benefit may be derived, in a prophylactic way, than from all the drugs that could be given.

Many professional men, like the laborious merchant, by hard work, sedentary habits, by neglecting to keep up a proper equilibrium between mental and physical labor—overworking the mind at the expense of the body—are overtaken by a similar train of ills, prominent among which stand incipient disorders of the liver, slight bronchial affections, occasional attacks of indigestion, frequent instances of defective action of the kidneys, and almost constant dryness of the skin : all harbingers of serious trouble, not far off in the future. Not feeling sufficiently indisposed to place himself under the care of his physician, yet conscious that he needs recreation, and something to give tone to his worn system, and to re-invigorate his exhausted energies, that professional man will be fortunate who, in seeking a resort during the summer for a few weeks of rest, shall find also, at the same time, a remedial agent already prepared to his hand, admirably adapted to remove those premonitory symptoms of very grave disease. During the past season a number of facts, bearing upon the above, were observed by us. The judicious administration of these waters, but particularly the sulphur, imparted a degree of vigor and freshness in such persons, that was truly gratifying; they felt, as it were, rejuvenated, and that they had a firmer hold upon life.

6

A third class, who will be saved from permanent and at last fatal disease, by a timely resort
to mineral springs, includes those ladies, old,
young, and middle aged, who have been living
inactive lives, and such as have been indulging
in irregularities in eating, sleeping, and in expos-
ing themselves to cold and dampness, and who
have produced by such habits an installment of
the earlier indications of some of the diseases
peculiar to females; such as paleness, loss of
appetite, debility, leucorrhœa, disorder of the
menstrual functions, etc., etc.

Finally, in all the walks of life, cases occur,
where there seems to be no active disease, but
where the person is troubled with languor, lassi-
tude, paleness, general weakness, and an indisposition to exertion, however slight, whether of
work or amusement—a condition this side of
hypochondriasis, but bordering upon and tending
toward it. Such a situation is as unpleasant, if
not as painful, as well-marked disease; but after
the use of the sulphur water for a few days, the
liver was excited to an active state, the dry skin
was rendered moist and soft, the kidneys were
aroused to an unusual secretion, the bowels were
regulated, the appetite became imperative—in
fact, the whole system was revolutionized, a keen

relish took the place of indifference, and the individual returned to his business with new zest—with an enthusiasm akin to that felt in the earlier years of manhood.

To such conditions of the body, mineral waters of the alterative class are singularly suited. One so afflicted might in vain resort to ordinary medication, but be speedily relieved by a remedy of "God's own composition" (as medicinal springs have been termed by Paracelsus)—reaching, as it does, the system in a state of perfect solution, it is absorbed, enters the blood-vessels, and by them is carried to every part, it reaches every tissue, every fiber, thus saturating, as it were, the entire organism.

Favorable as seems this comparison to mineral water, it may yet not be considered partial, extravagant, or unsupported by facts. It is but a just tribute to that Wisdom which arranged and combined the ingredients of these waters, and to that Goodness which sent their crystal streams sparkling to the surface, to be within man's reach, to freshen and to purify him, and to tempt him from the shrine of Bacchus to that of Hygeia.

APPENDIX.

Improvements for the Year 1859, at the Ohio White Sulphur Springs.

THE proprietors think that their accommodations are now such as to give entire satisfaction to the health and pleasure-seeking public, and are determined that nothing shall be left undone during the season to render guests comfortable, and to make their stay both agreeable and advantageous.

Invalids may rely upon every facility being furnished them for the use of the water internally, and for its application in the most approved forms of baths.

Telegraph Office.

At the Ohio White Sulphur Springs a Telegraph Office has been established, which will be open during the season, thus enabling visitors to communicate with all parts of the United States. Business men, more especially, will recognise the great importance of such an arrangement.

Buildings.

The improvements of the Springs during the present year have been extensive, consisting in a large Hotel, new Cottages, Bowling Alleys, Bath Houses, Steam Laundry, etc., etc., more than doubling former accommodations. A new Hotel, more than 200 feet in length, has been erected, furnishing parlors, suites of rooms, dining-hall, reception room, etc. This hotel, for size, elegance and adaptation to the purposes, is seldom surpassed. The dining-hall is commodious and easy of access; the reception room convenient, and the suites of rooms well arranged for comfort and retirement.

A LARGE ROOM FOR EVENING AMUSEMENTS has been provided. Surrounding this room, on three sides, is a tasteful porch, upon which open a number of bay windows, thus giving a complete ventilation; a consideration of much importance, both as it respects health and pleasure.

By reference to the engraving, it will be seen that the row of cottages upon a line with the Mansion House and Hotel, has been extended to twice its former length, while a number of two story cottages have been erected upon the southern aspect of the lawn, on the border of the grove.

Baths.

New Bath Houses have been built, and the most admirable arrangements for bathing instituted. A method has been adopted by which the water is heated in the bath tub. Under the old system, the water being raised to a high heat in the boiler or tank, most of the saline matter which it contained was deposited; but, with the present plan, heated by steam pipes in the bath tub while the person is using it, the water is applied with all its mineral ingredients to the surface.

Baths thus prepared resemble, as near as may be, those at Warm and Hot springs; and there can be no doubt but that the plan will at once recommend itself to all, but more especially to the medical profession, who often feel the great necessity of proper and efficient bathing facilities.

Steam Laundry.

The frequent difficulties met with at watering-places in getting the large amount of washing done, has induced the proprietor to erect a building exclusively for a laundry, where, by the aid of steam and machinery, the washing can be done with dispatch and without injury to the clothes.

Bowling Alleys.

The facilities for exercise and recreation have been much enlarged. In addition to the large Bowling Hall erected in 1858, another has been built near the river bank, which will afford room enough for all who may feel disposed to engage in such amusements.

Grounds, Lawn, Grove, etc.

· During the past year additions have been made to the grounds, and they have also been greatly improved and beautified. The grove, containing near one hundred acres, one of the most beautiful in Ohio, has been been laid off handsomely into walks and drives. As a woodland retreat from the summer sun, this grove will present many inducements to those in quest of out-door exercise and amusement.

The lawn, heretofore large and beautiful, has had, by a recent extension, added to it a number of fine walks and large shade trees, which, with its five sparkling springs, tasteful buildings and varied surface challenges the admiration of all, and may be compared favorably with that belonging to any watering-place in the country.

Livery Stable.

A livery stable, well supplied with horses and carriages, is attached to the Springs.

In addition to a drive two miles in length, which has been graded upon the estate, the country surrounding is varied and picturesque, and intersected with good roads for riding and driving.

Railroad Relations of the Ohio White Sulphur Springs.

By reference to the map it will be seen that the Ohio White Sulphur Springs are situated near the Capital and center of the State, and within a triangle of railroads, the boundaries of which are made by the Cleveland and Columbus R. R. from Columbus to Delaware; by the Springfield, Mt. Vernon & Pittsburg R. R. from Delaware to Milford Center; and by the Columbus, Piqua & Indiana R. R. from Milford Center to Columbus. It will be seen therefore, that the Springs are closely connected with two of the great thoroughfares from the East to the West.

The Springs have two Railroad Stations—one upon the Springfield, Mt. Vernon & Pittsburg R. R., and the other on the Columbus, Piqua & Indiana R. R. The former, *Ohio White Sulphur Station*, is 44 miles from Springfield, 5 miles from Delaware, and 5 miles from the Springs; the latter, *Pleasant Valley or Springs Station*, is 15 miles from Columbus and 10 miles from the Springs.

The three Railroads which thus surround the Springs, connect directly and indirectly with all the roads of Ohio and adjoining States, and in fact with all the great thoroughfares throughout the East and West; thus making this watering-place easy of access to all portions of our country. When we remember the fact that most of the great Mineral Springs of the United States are far removed from railroads and inaccessible by steam navigation, travelers in many instances having to ride from 40 to 60 miles over rough roads,—the admirable railroad relations of the Ohio White Sulphur Springs are a matter of satisfaction to the proprietor, while they must also be highly prized by all visitors.

CINCINNATI to Ohio White Sulphur Springs..........125 Miles.
Travelers may reach the Springs from Cincinnati,

Via Cincinnati, Hamilton & Dayton R. R. to Springfield, thence by the Springfield, Mt. Vernon & Pittsburg R. R. to the Ohio White Sulphur Station; or

Via Little Miami R. R. to Springfield, from Springfield, via Springfield, Mt. Vernon & Pittsburg R. R. to Ohio White Sulphur Station.

COLUMBUS to Ohio White Sulphur Springs..............18 Miles.
There being a regular Omnibus Line established from Columbus, passengers can take an Omnibus or Carriage direct to the Springs; or if they prefer to go by railway they can do so, either

Via the Columbus, Piqua & Indiana R. R. to Pleasant Valley or Springs Station; or

Via the Cleveland & Columbus R. R. to Delaware, thence 5 miles to the O. W. S. Sta'n. on the Springfield, Mt. Vernon & Pittsburg R.R.

DAYTON to Ohio White Sulphur Springs....................65 Miles.
Via Mad River R. R. to Springfield, and via Springfield, Mt. Vernon & Pittsburg R. R. to Ohio White Sulphur Station.

INDIANAPOLIS to Ohio White Sulphur Springs ....176 Miles.
Via Indiana Central, Dayton & Western and Mad River Railroads, to Springfield, from Springfield, via S., Mt. V. & P. R. R. to O. W. S. Station; or
Via Bellefontaine & Indiana R. R. to Union, thence via Columbus, Piqua & Indiana R. R. to Pleasant Valley or Springs Station.

PITTSBURG to Ohio White Sulphur Springs............227 Miles.
Via Pittsburg, Columbus & Cincinnati R. R. to Columbus; or
Via Pittsburg, Ft. Wayne & Chicago R. R. to Crestline, from Crestline via Cleveland & Columbus R. R. to Delaware, and from Delaware to the Ohio White Sulphur Station.

WHEELING to Ohio White Sulphur Springs............174 Miles.
Via Ohio Central Railroad to Columbus.

CHICAGO to Ohio White Sulphur Springs..................350 Miles.
Persons from Chicago and North-West will have a choice of routes to the Springs, either by way of Springfield, Urbana, Columbus or Delaware.

ZANESVILLE to Ohio White Sulphur Springs............77 Miles.
Via Central Ohio R. R. to Columbus, thence by Railroad or Omnibus.

LEXINGTON, KY. to Ohio White Sulphur Springs, 228 Miles.
Via Kentucky Central R. R. to Cincinnati, thence as above, C., H. & D. R. R. or L. M. R. R.

LOUISVILLE to Ohio White Sulphur Springs...........265 Miles.
Via Cincinnati or Indianapolis.

ST. LOUIS to Ohio White Sulphur Springs................436 Miles.
Via Cincinnati or Indianapolis.

DETROIT, MICH. to Ohio White Sulphur Springs, 227 Miles.
Via Toledo, Sandusky or Cleveland.

BUFFALO to Ohio White Sulphur Springs,...............296 Miles.
Via Cleveland and Delaware.

LAFAYETTE, IA. to Ohio White Sulphur Springs, 240 Miles.
Via Indianapolis & Union, to Pleasant Valley or Springs Station; or
Via Indianapolis, Dayton & Springfield, to Ohio White Sulphur Station.

TOLEDO to Ohio White Sulphur Springs,..................162 Miles.
Via Clyde and Springfield, to the Ohio White Sulphur Station.

TERRE HAUTE, IA. to Ohio White Sulphur Springs,
....**249 Miles.**
Via Indianapolis & Union, to Pleasant Valley or Springs Station; or
Via Indianapolis, Dayton & Springfield.

SANDUSKY to Ohio White Sulphur Springs,............**170 Miles.**
Via Springfield to Ohio White Sulphur Station; or
Via Urbana, thence by Columbus, Piqua & Indiana R. R.

STEUBENVILLE, O. to Ohio White Sulphur Springs,
....**168 Miles.**
Via Columbus or Delaware.

CLEVELAND to Ohio White Sulphur Springs,........**113 Miles.**
Via Cleveland & Columbus R. R. to Delaware, thence to Ohio White
Sulphur Station.

CHILLICOTHE to Ohio White Sulphur Springs........**63 Miles.**
Via Columbus by Coach, or via Marietta & Cincinnati and Little
Miami Railroads to Springfield.

				MILES.
NEW YORK,	to Ohio White Sulphur Springs			680
NEW ORLEANS,	"	"	"	1565
PHILADELPHIA,	"	"	"	586
BOSTON,	"	"	"	794
BALTIMORE,	"	"	"	544
WASHINGTON CITY,	"	"	"	566
MEMPHIS,	"	"	"	765
CUMBERLAND,	"	"	"	366

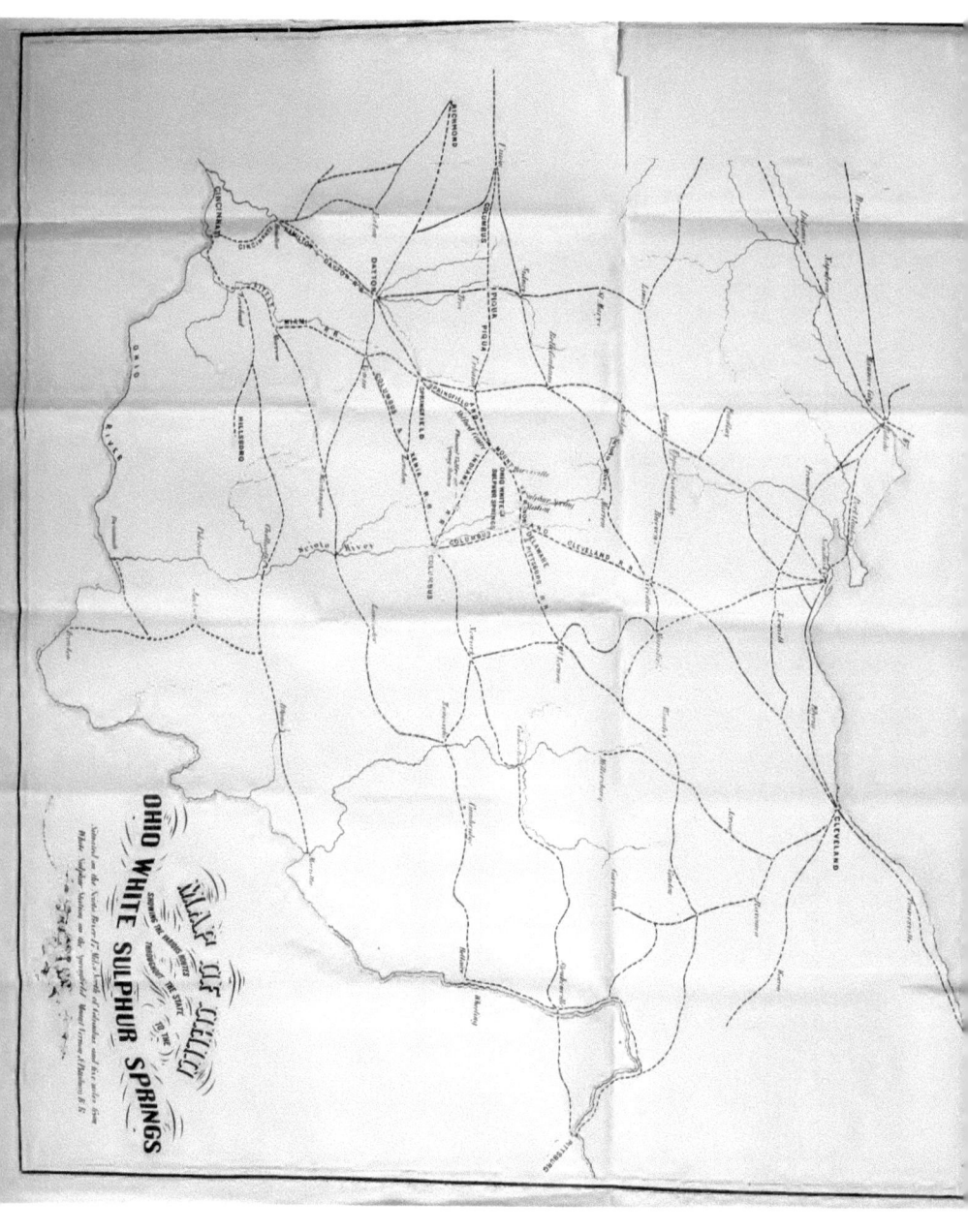

MAP OF THE
OHIO WHITE SULPHUR SPRINGS